Two Strangers On The Bed

Kotra Siva Rama Krishna

Published by Kotra Siva Rama Krishna, 2022.

This is a work of fiction. Similarities to real people, places, or events are entirely coincidental.

TWO STRANGERS ON THE BED

First edition. October 27, 2022.

Copyright © 2022 Kotra Siva Rama Krishna.

ISBN: 979-8215313589

Written by Kotra Siva Rama Krishna.

Also by Kotra Siva Rama Krishna

Two Strangers On The Bed
A Girl's Conflict
Enna
Strawberry
Dusk
Just Relax!
Delicious Predicament
Nirupama
Half Opened Doors
Lovenest
Moonshine
Scarecrow
Closed Doors
Disturbed
Handfuls of Sand
Mansion of Illusions
Rain Flower
Rose Garden
Sand Dunes
Snow Flower
Split Personality
Being Possessed
Objection Sustained
House of Delusions
Rustle in the Leaves

Sasikala
Amaswitha
English Grammar Simplifier
Wisps of Smoke

License Notes

Disclaimer

The concept, plot, story, characters and everything in this novel are only fiction and emerged only out of the imagination of this author. If anything in this novel even a small part of it resembles, similar or identical to any living or dead or to any literature, anywhere in the world even remotely it is only coincidental and this author has no knowledge whatsoever of it and cannot take any responsibility for the same.

About me

I am an Indian English writer write mostly fiction books and so far I have written thirty books out of which twenty eight books are romantic, psychological thrillers and the remaining two are non-fiction books, Body, Mind and You and English Grammar Simplifier. The word count of my books range from 15,000 to 3,50,000 and the total word count of all my books is more than 30,00,000 (Thirty Lakhs Words). I have a weakness, I don't get the feeling that I wrote the book if someone else edits the same, so I am my own editor to all my books. As such there is a pretty chance that you may come across grammatical, verbal mistakes, incongruities and inconsistencies while going through my books, then please pardon me and go ahead. I am always open as much as possible when it comes to sexual narrations in my books as I think sex is very main and natural characteristic not just in human beings but in all other creatures also. So you can find sexual narrations in my books graphical, absolute and complete. My heart-felt thanks to all those who have been purchasing my books all along, encouraging me and supporting me.

The story briefly

It was Sameera's, a twenty two years young and married girl's strong desire to be the opposite sex and see how everything is to the opposite sex and Praomod, a twenty three years young and married man with a son, also has the same wish as much strongly as hers and it was just co-incidence that they both studied in the same class, same college and knew each other. It was also just co-incidence, that after they settled in their lives, they both met during a journey in a bus and shared the things of their lives including their strong desire to be the opposite sex and to enjoy everything as an opposite sex. Just before fell into sleep during that journey in that bus side by side in their seats, they thought in themselves how nice it would be if they become the other person, the opposite sex. To their shock and astonishment, when they woke up they found themselves in the other's body. Even they could enjoy being the opposite sex by staying in the other's body, they just did not understand how it has happened and did not know how long it would be so. Then staying in the other's body, they went to the other's home instead of theirs, managed themselves with the knowledge they obtained from the other all the time feeling confusion and uneasiness but not without enjoying their strongly cherished desire to become the opposite sex. How long they enjoyed their staying in the opposite sex like that and when their souls changed their places into their respective bodies again and how; is the story 'They Were Strangers To Themselves!' a hot, hot romantic thriller with 23 thousand words count.

Two Strangers on the Bed

It was one hour or so after the bus started moving and Pramod knew it would take nearly ten hours or so to the bus to reach his destination. The bus was almost empty except two passengers on the rear side. It was evening four and Pramod put himself reading some ebook in his smart-phone by the time the bus stopped in a bus station. Pramod could not remain without observing the proceedings then and the two passengers who were in the bus till that moment alighted from it and some three passengers entered into it.

"I think I know you." The twenty two years or so young girl, who was one of the passengers entered into the bus came straight to him and slumped herself on the seat beside him.

"I am just thinking like that." With a smile on his lips Pramod said. "After studying together three years in the same class in the same college, it is nearly impossible not to know each other, is it is not?" There was the same happy and surprising expression in his face reflecting hers. It was indeed impossible to forget Sameera who was the most beautiful woman in their college at that time.

"Of course, you are right!" her laughter was mellifluous and he could not remain without observing minutely her youthful and beautiful figure.

It was very much surprising to him that she came like that, slumped beside him and started talking so! Not just he, almost all the boys in the college used to observe and try to make friendship with her while they were studying in the college. But it was only he who never tried to let his interest on her to be known to anyone.

"You never used to talk with anyone, a reserved type! I think it was only you who never has shown any interest in me."

While he was thinking furiously what to talk she said again. That meant he really could manage that his interest on her not to be known to her.

"Really you did observe that much of me?" the surprise was genuine in the face of Pramod. "You also very much reserved type and never appeared to show interest on anyone."

"But I showed some interest on you." the serious expression in her face was surprised Pramod. "Because you appeared handsome to me and on some occasions I wanted to talk with you. Before doing anything like that, our college education was over and we parted our ways. Anyhow........." once again her laughter was mellifluous "...............just because mine was mere interest on you and nothing more I did not feel much at all."

"No problem whatsoever." Pramod also laughed. "But as you are open like this to me I also want to open with you. Just like the other boys, probably even more, I also was attracted towards you. I also did some research on you and came to know some of the details about you."

But he did not want to say what he came to know about her because it was not very much glorious. She was the eldest daughter in a poor family which comprised one sister and one brother. Her father was doing a very small job, her family was struggling a lot for maintenance and in fact looking forward for her completing education and join in a job.

"It is a surprise to me! You never appeared like a boy to show interest on girls like that." She smiled.

"Unless you were such beautiful..........." he did not know how he was saying it like that. "..........I would not have bothered like that. Anyhow, no problem! Long before I found out mine also was just interest on you and nothing more."

There was some silence between them both and both of them were observing the nature outside while the bus was moving fast. Just minutes before the bus crossed the concrete jungle and entered onto the road which was laid through the green fields.

"I really like observing the greenery in this way." She said with a slow voice.

"It would be even more wonderful if you observe that sitting beside the window. Please come into my seat." Pramod got off from the seat he sat.

Pramod reserved his seat in the internet and she bought her seat at the counter in the bus-station.

"But you would have reserved that window seat particularly for the pleasure of observing outside." The gathered frowns on her forehead were also beautiful while she was saying that.

"You sacrificed the pleasure of sitting at a window seat even there are so many window seats vacant now." He smiled and said. "Its a pleasure to me to give you the pleasure to observe the nature through the window."

Then it just took seconds to both of them to change their seats. Once again there was silence between them both until the bus passed through the greenery and entered into concrete jungle again.

"What you are doing now? Still studying?" suddenly breaking that silence and looking into his face, she asked him.

"I put a stop to my studies when I was selected as a bank manager. I really did not expect but when I have been qualified in the competitive exam for manager for a nationalised bank I could not deny that." There was little regret in his face as he did not like much what he did.

"Really a nice thing in my opinion!" She smiled. "But it seems that you have not enjoyed what you did."

"You are right. I really did not like to stop pursuing my English literature in M.A. and do Ph.D also in that. My family was not in very much financial need also at that time. But everyone said getting a job as a manager in a nationalised bank is not a small thing. I was sort of hypnotised and joined in that job."

"Really it was so?" she laughed her mellifluous laughter gain. "If it was so, why did you apply to that competitive exam? Even you applied for it, why did you write that exam that much better? If you did not write it better, you need not have done the thing you were not interested in."

"I have applied for that competitive exam just casually along with my friends. Even more casually I wrote the exam without any idea that I do write it that much better that I would be called for an interview. When I have attended that interview......"

"............you have no idea that you would do it better and select for the job." She interrupted him and said sighing heavily. "I know how much painful it is to do things which we don't like."

"I did another very much painful thing which I did not like at all."

She knitted her brows and looked into his face with a questioning expression.

"I got married." He too sighed heavily. "I have become a target to the fathers of the girls once I settled in a good job like that and it did not take much time that my marriage was performed with a girl."

"Sooner or later you have to be married. What that much worrying in getting married once you are settled in a good job also?" there was again a questioning expression in her face. "Were you in love with someone? Wanted to marry some other girl but that was not possible and have married to your wife?"

"It was not at all so." He smiled but still with frowns and regretting expression in his face. "But I don't want to be married at the age of twenty three and become a father also just by the age of twenty four itself!"

"Congratulations! Now you are a father also." the frowns on her face were cleared and she smiled. "Is it is a son or daughter?"

"I am the father of one year aged son." He once again sighed heavily.

"At the age of twenty five my dad has me, my sister and my brother, I came to know" she said with an admonishing expression in her face. "It was not very much horrifying and surprising! You are indeed lucky that you got a son. You have to enjoy your life."

"You are right I agree." He nodded his head with a plain expression in his face. "When my wife also is not disappointing, even though she is not as much beautiful as you are but beautiful and youthful, I say you are absolutely right. I am trying to make change in my mindset."

"Don't let that poor girl sad because of your nonsense interest. She has every right to be happy in her life along with you." With little angry expression in her face she said.

"Even I am not happy altogether with my life, I am not thinking I am making her unhappy for anything." He said and once again sighed heavily. "Anyhow I check and see and if I am really making her unhappy for anything, I make amends."

"That's indeed a good idea!" her laughter was always mellifluous but it was just for few seconds then. "You told about yourself. Don't you want to know about me?" suddenly her face became serious.

"Who said I don't want?" he knitted his brows "I am just waiting for the opportunity to ask. Pour yourself."

She sighed heavily and leaned back in the seat "In fact I don't know what to say. My life also is not as per my wish and will."

"Could not you marry the one you loved?" he paused for a moment before saying again "But you did not appear to me ever someone like fell in love type."

"Assumption right!" she made a pathetic laugh. "But I did not want to marry someone who is not only aged more than ten years to me but a widower with a daughter."

"I am sorry, I am indeed sorry." He indeed felt unhappy on hearing that but did not feel surprise on hearing that. That widower must be a rich person influenced her family with lot of money which made even Sameera also agree to that. "May I hope atleast that your family problems have been solved with your marriage?"

"It seems that you did enough research on my family." She nodded her head. "Yes, with my marriage my family problems have been solved absolutely. My husband is not only a very rich man but he has very generous nature also. As he has no family of his own my family has become his only family and he felt as much happy as he is helping his own family in helping my family."

There was silence once again and Pramod remained silent as he did not know what more to ask.

"It is a regret that I could not marry someone matching with my age but I cannot say I am not at all happy with my husband. He has a handsome personality and he loves me and likes me a lot. He always feels that he is so much fortunate to get me as his wife."

"Then I must say.........." with a sort of firmness in his voice Pramod said. "........you should happily compromise with your life. We cannot have our lives we want in every way."

"You are right.........you are right..........." Sameera nodded her head and about to say something but then the bus was suddenly stopped and they heard the announcement of the conductor.

"The bus got into some damage and it takes sometime to get it repaired. You people take rest in the nearby dhaba in the meanwhile."

It was indeed their luck that the bus got into repair near a dhaba and the few passengers in that bus walked towards that dhaba at that time and Pramod and Sameera also were among them.

"Both of us also have to be compromised to some extent in our lives." After slumping themselves in two chairs at a table Pramod said after ordering for coffee for both of them.

"But not very much need to be compromised" Sameera said. "Even it is somehow odd to marry a widower with a child aging ten years old to me, I must say that I am happy with my husband. Moreover I cannot say how my family condition would have been now without my husband's help."

"You are right!" by then they have been served with coffee in two cups and Pramod started sipping his while Sameera preferred to leave hers still on the table. "Except I have become a family man at the age of twenty three itself against my wish and will, my life also is so much happy with my wife, only son and parents." He said in between the sips. "At present I am living only with my wife and son as my parents are living in our native village where we have lands."

"I don't know why but I want to share some of my things with you. For a long time I am waiting for someone, some opposite sex, to share my exact feelings, wishes and desires. And you are appearing to be exact the same." Sameera also took her coffee cup into her right hand and started sipping it.

"It is really very much surprising to me!" Pramod said and his surprise was amply reflected in his face also. "We know each other very little and both of us agreed what we have got on each other in those days was just interest! Still you want to share your things with me."

"Yes, of course." She took a sip of the coffee and put it on the table before balancing herself on it on her arms. "That someone need not be a very close friend to me but has some patience to hear my feelings and understand me and tell me what he is thinking."

"I have that patience and certainly can be that exact one to share your feelings, understand you and tell you about my thinking. But..........." he paused for a second before saying again. "............why cannot you share the same with your husband? You yourself said that he loves you and likes you a lot."

"No, no. My husband does not fit in that exact one but you fit." With a fixed expression in her face Sameera said.

"I don't know how much of time we have got to be together like this." There came a fixed expression in the face of Pramod also. "But I am very much interested to hear whatever you are going to say. Just pour your heart."

"But you must not laugh and you must not hate me after hearing me." Suddenly the expression in her face was turned into troubling and uneasy.

"Very much surprising! I just cannot understand what you really want to share with me." Feeling puzzlingly Pramod said. "I cannot say about my reaction after hearing you. I want to be frank that it depends on what I am going to hear. But my promise rests! I am ready to hear whatever you are going to say and tell you what I am thinking. If you have no objection............"

"Certainly I have no objection. I already told you I am just waiting for someone like you." a fixed expression came into her face also. "For a long time I want so desperately to be a man. How it is to be a man rather than a woman? The thought itself is very much thrilling and interesting to me."

"Considering the privileges the men folk do have and the convenience of their body structure comparing with women, it is not surprising that some women want to be men. There is nothing to laugh at you or hate you because of your simple wish." Pramod sighed heavily and leaned back in the chair. "I hoped that you were going to tell me something very much thrilling and interesting."

"You did not go into the core of what I have said." She dragged the chair even more near to the table and stooped even more and balanced her arms once again on the table. "I want to be a man, to know how the pleasure in fucking rather than being fucked! How a man feels putting his thing in a woman and moving it. How his feeling and pleasure while he is enjoying each and every part of a woman. Especially I want to be a man to know and enjoy that."

Pramod's face was filled with shock and surprise! "Did I really hear you or just imagined all this?" his shock and surprise were amply reflected in his face also.

"You heard me right. There is no mistaking in it." With an uneasy expression in her face she said and leaned back in the chair. "There is no chance that I can be a man and know about that. You are a man and you already fucked a woman. Tell me how it is?"

"Still I ask the same question to you." Pramod said and the shock and surprise in his face were just so. "Why don't you ask about it to your own husband? He fucks you quite often and tells you about it."

"I just don't know how he feels if I ask him like this. I have to live along with him all my life and if a different sort of opinion sets in him on me because of my asking so, my life becomes difficult to me. There is no problem in whatever type of opinion you get on me just because we are not going to live together." Sameera said.

"I understand! You are right." With a smile on his lips Pramod nodded his head.

"You just don't know how much I want that to know. Sometimes I so much desire to become a man by transgender operation."

"Even there is a chance like that, it never can be made you fully understand how a man feels then." Pramod said with a smile. "And narrating about the sexual intercourse of me as a man also may not completely satisfy your craving."

"You are right............you are right.............I agree." Sameera nodded her head "But I am feeling happy to express my wish daringly like this with you. What you are thinking after hearing my odd wish?"

"I just cannot say but there can never be more co-incidence than this!" frowns gathered on Pramod's forehead and his face was with full of surprise. "I have been also wishing in the same way as you do. I also just want to know, how the opposite sex feels, I mean how a woman feels, while she is being fucked. I exactly want to know how it is being fucked rather than fucking. But I did not wait like you for an opposite sex to know about it as you did."

"Really, really you feel like that! You want to know how a woman feels while a man is engaging with her in sex, enjoying her beauty inch by inch and fucking her putting his thing into her?" her face was suddenly with full of surprise.

"Every point of it I want to know. I feel very much thrilling thinking about a woman having sex with a man."

"Then have you also felt thrilled to share your desire like this with me?"

"Of course, I have felt thrill to share my feeling with you. But long before itself I shared this with my wife and told her how much I wished to be a woman to know about it."

"Then what she said?" Sameera knitted her brows together.

"She told me about her experience while I was doing that to her. She said there would be pleasure all over to her. I am sorry I cannot explain everything she said to me. But just hearing never completely satisfies our craving. To know exactly how a woman feels then, I have to become an absolute woman and it is never possible." Pramod said sighing heavily.

"You are right. I also have to become a man to know about it in full and that is just impossible." Sameera also sighed heavily. "But I have some satisfaction by daringly sharing my desire like this with you. And if you tell me how exactly it is while a man is fucking a woman, my craving can be some more satisfied."

"While doing that; a man feels pleasure with every fibre of his being. The main pleasure points to a man at the nipples on his chest. If the woman teases them with her fingers or tongue the pleasure he enjoys will be more than real fucking." Pramod started feeling a sort of pleasure in explaining that to her.

"I really don't know about it." Once again frowns gathered on the forehead of Sameera.

"The most attracting things to a man in a woman are her breasts and I don't think that it needs to be told to you. If the woman provides chance, he can enjoy every part of her including her main organ. Unfortunately most of the women don't agree to it."

"Yes, you are right. I too don't agree to it." Remembering her own experience with her husband Anurag, Sameera said.

"But once he released himself into the woman, man lasts all his strength. Once the release is over there will be no desire in him for sometime. He just wants to go away from the woman until he feels for it again."

"Quite contrarily, a woman wants the man with her after his release also. She just wants him to stay on the top of her for some more time and whenever I want that to be so, my husband always obliges."

"Your husband is a very understanding type! My wife also wants me to be so but I never agree." Pramod said. "Now tell me about your exact way of behaving and feeling while your husband is doing that to you."

"I cannot say, just because I am not very much enjoying my sexual life with him. All the time I just want it to come to a finish."

"Very wrong and sad on your part I must say." Pramod angrily said. "Anyhow it seems to me that you don't like to be a woman at all. Is it has become impossible to you to have sex with a man?"

"It is not at all so." Sameera nodded her head in negation. "I want to be a man and know how a man feels while doing that to a woman but I can enjoy sex as a woman also. But as I have to marry him against my will and wish, I just cannot cooperate with him in all respects."

"That is indeed very much wrong on your part. You have to change yourself."

"I am trying. But I just cannot change." Her face was filled with a helpless expression.

"You should try even more seriously to change yourself as your husband is such a good character and helped your family a lot."

"Alright, alright. I do try even more seriously from now on to change myself." She laughed.

"Just like in your case.........." Pramod paused for a second before continuing as if to reiterate whatever he was going to say. "...............I also just want to know how a woman feels then. I enjoy sex as a man also. I never regret that I born as a man."

After that, they talked even more about their college days, families and other things until they have been left with nothing to talk anymore and there was silence between them both for some seconds and then the conductor of the bus came to them and said. "Repairing of the bus is over. We can resume our journey again."

After making themselves comfortably in the seats as they were before alighting from the bus, Pramod and Sameera looked into each other's faces with curious expressions and smiles. It has become complete night by that time and only small lights were going on in the bus making them able to see only the outlines of their figures.

"Thank god! I am happy that I shared my strongest desire like that with you. I am still feeling a lot to be a man to know about it. How nice if I become you, a very handsome personality .... "she was once again feeling her strong desire but her eyes were closed before she completed that sentence.

Pramod just remained staring into the beautiful face of her. Considering her glamorous figure, no one could guess that she has such desire in her. Even more audaciously she expressed her wish like that at him!

But what a surprising and shocking co-incidence! How he was also feeling to become his opposite sex! Or every human being wished to be both just like the both of them? He did not understand and he could not dwell on that more either as he was also feeling too much sleepy and he did not know when he fell asleep. But before fell into sleep, he also thought how nice it would be if he would become her, a very beautiful woman, to know about it.

x x x

By the time Pramod woke up it was complete morning and he could see greenery outside through the window as the bus once again entered into the fields. But he suddenly remembered something! He has given his window seat to Sameera and after the repairing of the bus also he let her sit in that window seat. After that he saw her falling into sleep, he also slipped into deep sleep and only now he woke up. In the meanwhile when they have changed their seats again he could not remember at all. Feeling surprise, he looked at the seat beside him and he received shock!

He was sleeping in the seat in which Sameera supposed to be. If he was sleeping in that where she has gone? How it was possible to him to be in both seats? How he could think and feel like this while sleeping like that? Then he automatically looked at his lap.

He found the handbag of Sameera in his lap and he was holding it with both of his hands. Not just that, the hands which were holding that handbag then were Sameera's not his. He just could not understand anything at all. With that surprise and shocking state, he rummaged in the handbag expecting a small mirror. His expectation did not go wrong as just like some women, Sameera also kept a small mirror in her handbag. With shivering hands he took that mirror upto his face and looked into that. Then he got his lifetime shock!

He was looking at the face of Sameera in that small mirror! He did not know how it has happened and how it could be possible but instantly he understood one thing! His soul was transferred into the body of Sameera. Even everything is possible in supernatural way, he did not think her soul also in the same body then. If his assumption was right, her soul was transferred into his body.

He did not want to think about that transferring of souls then as there would be lot of time to do that later. First thing he need to do was making her also understand the point. Once she was also made understand the issue both of them have to think about it together. Thinking like that, he tapped on her right cheek slowly and while she was struggling to wake up he said hurriedly "Don't open your eyes. First try to understand what I am going to say and then only open them."

"What the bloody hell you are talking? First let me know what it is. I cannot remain closing my eyes like this for long." Irritation filled her face.

"A very surprising thing took place! I just don't know how it has become possible but our souls were changed bodies while we were sleeping in the night." With a slow but clear voice, coming so near to her right ear Pramod said.

"Certainly you lost your mind and imagining things!" with the same irritation she opened her eyes and could not refrain herself from yelling when she has seen her own self in the other seat attracting the few passengers attention towards them. "How it has become possible to me to be in both places?" her voice shivered while saying that.

"You are not in both places. It is my body in the place you are now. Just look yourself into this mirror and that confirms everything." Then he put the hand mirror against her face.

She yelled once again and it made the few passengers in that bus to look at them with surprise once more. "Yes, its you! Its absolutely you!" The shiver in her voice was increased even more.

"Now do you believe that I did not imagine the whole thing? Our souls have been changed their places! Mine into yours and yours into mine." he said and by that time he stopped feeling surprise and started thinking what has to be done.

"But...........but.............I just don't know............what we should do now?" her face was with complete shock and surprise and she was not able to understand anything still.

"Changing of our souls like this is not a dream but its a fact! We need to do lot of thinking together for our future actions. We need to alight from the bus in the next stop, go to some peaceful place and think about everything. Shocking and surprising ourselves is not going to solve anything."

"As you said" Sameera nodded her head and her voice was very weak.

x x x

"How a phenomenon like this has happened I just cannot understand! Even in movies and books also I never came across something like this! How souls change bodies like this?" Sameera said.

As Pramod suggested, both of them were alighted from the bus in the coming stop. It was a town and without much difficulty they could find a park nearby and luckily they found a bench to sit and talk without any people around.

"I agree, just before going into sleep I thought how nice it would be if I become you. A handsome, young man! Just because of that this soul change could happen?" Sameera said again. By then she also assimilated whatever has taken place however much it was unbelievable to her.

"Might it happened like that just because.........." Pramod sighed heavily. "...............just before going into sleep, I also thought in the same way. How nice it would be if I become you. A beautiful and glamorous woman! As we both desired and wished so strongly in the same way at the same time to be the other person, the opposite sex, this phenomenon took place."

"But I cannot go to my home with your body and you cannot go to my home with my body!" The gathered frowns were deepened even more on her forehead. "What should we do now?"

"To think about that particularly we both assembled here now." Pramod paused for a second looking into her face straight. "Yes, you are absolutely right! We cannot go into our respective homes with different bodies. We would not be even allowed into our homes and no one does believe our story. The only present solution to our problem is; I do go to your home with your body and you have to go my home with my body."

"But how can we manage in our homes without knowing anything about each other?" she said but some understanding has come into her also.

"Then we are going to be known about each other fully. You tell about your husband, your life there and the rest. I tell you about my life and the rest. Then it would not become that much difficult to us to manage ourselves in different homes."

"Yes, it is appearing reasonable. For the present I too cannot see any other solution except that to our problem." She said but once again frowns gathered on her forehead. "It may not be difficult to you to manage yourself in my home after knowing about me fully. But how can I manage myself as a bank manager? A lot need to be known to discharge duties as a bank manager."

"That's a problem I agree. But there is a solution to that problem also." He smiled "Just tell the assistant manager Susmitha that you have got some problem with your memory and you needed her help in full. She sure would help you and you don't face even a little problem then."

"Alright" Sameera nodded her head still feeling uneasily at the idea to work in the bank.

"But there is a problem with that Susmitha. She has a problem with her husband and pestering me to have it with her. If anyone else in my place he would have because that Susmitha is a beautiful woman but I am not. It will be little cumbersome to you with her but presently I cannot see any other way to manage yourself in the bank."

"My god! Really horrible!" Sameera nodded her head with a helpless expression. "But when there is no other way, what we can do? Alright I try to manage."

"Now I tell you about my wife, about my home everything in detail. Listen carefully. If you face any problem, just phone to me and I sort that out." It took nearly half an hour to him to explain everything about him to her. "In fact I attended a seminar and have been returning to my home. My home is not very far from here and you can go there by an auto. If you remember everything I said, it will not be difficult to manage yourself in my home and in the bank."

Sameera nodded her head and said. "I have been returning from my parents' home which is in the town of the bus-stop where I got into this bus. I need to go another ten kilometres to reach my home. In fact the next stop to this stop is my bus stop. I explain everything about myself to you. In your case it is not going to be as much difficult as to me." Then the time she has taken to explain everything about herself to him was less than he took.

"Wonderful indeed! You are right. My position is not going to be as much difficult as yours." Pramod said.

"Shall we start our respective journeys then? You to my home and I to your home with changed bodies?" Sameera got off from the bench and asked him.

"Absolutely! But for the convenience we both do one thing." Pramod also got off from the bench he sat and said looking into her face. "We tell everyone that we have got a sudden memory problem and cannot remember everything in a clear way. Then the mistakes we do without knowledge about the other can be easily covered."

"Wonderful idea indeed!" Sameera laughed but her laughter was not mellifluous as she was in the body of Pramod but just in seconds her face became serious and she asked with gathered frowns. "But how long it would be like this? When we can come into our respective bodies again?"

"I don't have even a vaguest idea on that but I want to say something here." Suddenly there came a fixed expression on Pramod's face. "Both of us strongly desired and wished to be the opposite sex and god has given us a way to get it fulfilled. Without bothering how long we have to be in this way, we try to enjoy our present condition which we desired so much."

"You are absolutely right!" the frowns gathered on her forehead were cleared.

"Now is the time to go to our respective destinations." He started to move away from that place.

"Just a moment!" for the first time Sameera hold the hand of Pramod and stopped him. "We can visit each other's homes and talk with each other. We can introduce ourselves as friends to our family."

"I think there will be no problem." After we seconds thinking Pramod said. "Susmitha quite often visits our home and my wife never misunderstood our relation. If your husband also doesn't get suspicion on you.........."

"No chance at all." Sameera laughed. "You just don't know what a nice guy is my husband. You can know about him in full only after meeting with him."

"Alright then. Now we proceed with our journey." Pramod said.

Then they both moved away from that place.

x x x

The uneasy feeling in Pramod was increased more and more along with the thrill feeling while he was entering into the house of Sameera with her body. Even it was shocking, surprising and quite uncomfortable, he has the thrill feeling that he could be the opposite sex which he desired and wished to be for a long time. He has to be seen how he would be received in the house! Even Sameera said that the welcome would be great to him, he was still feeling quite uneasy.

"Mom, you came!" a one year aged girl came running to Pramod and enveloped his legs with both of her hands.

"Yes, I came my dear!" he took that small girl into his hands, heaved her up and kissed on her right cheek. "It seems that you thought of me a lot."

"You are right. She thought about you a lot and has been worrying herself. But it is not your fault. You asked her a lot to come along with you but she did not agree."

Pramod remained looking at that six feet tall figure who was talking with her then. Even he was aged ten years old to Sameera, he was appearing quite handsome! Except the point that he was a widower with a one year aged daughter, he was alright! A woman can be happy with him on the bed also.

"Still I should not have gone like that without her." Considering him in the same way she said. "How is everything with you? Is everything comfortable?" she put that girl on the floor there and came near to him. "Rajani is a very naughty girl and she would have put you to lot of trouble in these two days or so." Sameera told him about her step daughter also in full.

"As much naughty as you are afraid! But you know very well if we let her play video games in cell phone, she would not trouble us much."

"But it is dangerous to let her play video games all along, don't you know?" she came even near to him and put her both hands around his neck. "I promise to you it is the last time that I go anywhere without her."

There was lot of surprise in his face as it was the very first time that she was doing so to him. "I am feeling very happy hearing you in this way." He also put his hands around her.

"There are things I need to share with you. When I have freshened myself up, we both sit together and talk." Pramod said and relieved himself from his hold after relieving him.

"Can you postpone that till the evening? I have to attend an urgent meeting in the office and I cannot postpone that." Looking at Pramod with a pleading expression in his face Anurag asked.

"I can postpone that till the morning if you want." Pramod laughed and said. "Finish your routine till the night of the day with a peaceful mind and then we can talk everything with open hearts."

"Alright dear!" he kissed on her right cheek before moving away from that place.

Pramod looked around to see what Rajani was doing then and she was in the hands of a fifty years aged woman.

"In these two days, I did not fail to come and look after your daughter. Only because of that sir could go to office peacefully." She said.

"I know that." Pramod remembered what Sameera has said about that fifty years aged woman, the servant maid in their home. "And thank you very much for that."

Then he moved towards the bedroom remembering what Sameera said about the house and it has not become difficult to him to locate that.

x x x

"You just don't know how much we both have been waiting for you." As soon as Sameera entered into the house with Pramod body, Pramod's wife Purnima came to her and put her both hands around her neck.

What Pramod said about Purnima was absolutely true! Purnima was not only youthful and attractive but beautiful also.

"It was only two days that I was away from you, need you feel this much for it?" pretending irritation in his face Sameera asked her.

"I cannot say anything about that." She left her hold around Sameera and said. "But I cannot remain without bothering for you if you are absent like that. Very seldom you go away from me leaving me all alone in the house."

"That is indeed nice!" Sameera put her both hands around the neck of Purnima and kissed on her both cheeks. "In fact I also feel in the same way to leave you and go away. Anyhow where is our son and what he is doing?"

"I have to give my cell phone to him to make him not to ask about you. You can find him in our bedroom and now it is your responsibility to take that cell phone from him and give it to me."

With a smile on her lips Sameera moved away from that place and into the adjoining room where she found one year or so aged boy playing something in the cell phone on the bed. As soon as he found Sameera there in Pramod body, he left the cell phone on the bed itself and came running to Sameera. As if it was best available opportunity, Purnima went to the bed and took the cell phone from there.

"I know that you do worry about me like this. So I came early." Sameera said. "I stay all this day in the home itself and go to the bank only on tomorrow."

"It is indeed very happy news!" laughing loudly Purnima said. "We can talk a lot in between ourselves."

"You are right! And I have to tell you one important thing also here."

"Tell me then what it is? I am very much eager to hear." With a curious expression in her face, Purnima asked Sameera.

"First let me refresh myself. Then I tell you." After saying so Sameera tried to walk away from that place but suddenly she was in confusion! Where was bathroom in that house? Pramod did not tell her about it at all. This house was appearing too big a one to locate it easily.

"Why did you fell in thinking? Go and refresh yourself." Looking at him with gathered frowns Purnima said.

"Where, where is bathroom in our house?" without looking into her face with complete uneasiness in her Sameera asked.

"Pramod dear, what happened to you?" Purnima came near to him and put her both hands around her neck and asked looking into Sameera's face "You forgot where our bathroom in our house?"

"I am thinking that it is better to tell about that something now itself." With the same uneasy expression in her face Sameera said. "While I was returning from the seminar I fell into deep sleep in the bus. Something happened to me in that deep sleep, that I cannot remember certain things after I woke up! That is what I want to tell you."

"My god! Is it is true?" the frowns gathered in the face of Purnima were thickened even more and anxiousness blanketed her face.

"It appears very strange to hear but it is absolutely true." The uneasiness was just so in the face of Sameera.

"I don't know.....I don't know what to say......" nodding her head helplessly Purnima said "But you are a bank manager! How you can do that job with a problem like this?"

"That is what I am also worrying! Anyhow I decided to take the help of that Susmitha until I recovery my memory fully. But I just don't know how to be got cured from this problem."

"We need to go to a psychiatrist Pramod, that only can solve this problem." Even in that shocking and surprising situation also Purnima took a decision. "We have to do that as soon as possible."

"Indeed a best idea! But first show me the bathroom. Once I finished my bath, we talk together."

Then it took ten minutes or so to Sameera to finish her bath and entered into the bedroom where Pramod' wife and son were waiting. Sameera did not face any problem in finding it as it was the same room into which Purnima took Sameera before where Pramod's son was playing with cell phone.

x x x

"I made Prathap to sleep and put him in the cradle there so we can talk peacefully. Now tell me everything!" Purnima said putting her both hands around Sameera's neck and kissing on her right cheek when Sameera reached beside her on the bed.

"Very nice thing you did!" Sameera kissed straight on Purnima's lips.

However much unbelievable, however much inconvenient and dumbfounding, Sameera was feeling very much happy as her strong desire was getting fulfilled in this way. She was an absolute man now, feeling as a man and now could have sex as a man! While taking bath she observed the body she was in and even she has seen the nude body of her husband on some occasions, she was appalled seeing the private parts of Pramod' body. Pramod has no habit to shave his private part and there was dense black hair! His penis was rather simple and small one covered by that black hair but while she was rubbing that part also there was some stirring and it stood up! It stood up to its full length! Then it was just like the one, her husband's! Her heart was with full of thrill feeling but just in seconds it flattened again.

Now also, in the warm hug of Purnima, she was feeling stirring there and she knew that thing was getting up. She understood how a man would feel while he was with full of sexual desire! Her immediate thinking was to fuck Purnima then and there but it seemed that Purnima has no such idea at that time.

"Now tell me dear! What exactly took place? What things you cannot remember? We are lucky that you did not forget your home and family also." Once again Purnima's face was with full of anxiousness.

"You are right! I thank god for that." Sameera laughed but her face suddenly became serious. "I too don't know what exactly has taken place. While travelling I fell into deep sleep. As it was night also there was nothing to feel surprise in it but when I woke up I felt completely different. Then I tried to remember certain things but I could not. After lot of probing I understood that I have got some problem with my memory and cannot remember certain things."

"I heard about people who have forgotten entirely and even about themselves also. But it is first time to me to know forgetting only certain issues!"

"I just cannot explain how it is so!" pretending a helpless expression in her face Sameera said. "But are not we fortunate that I did not forget everything?"

"Absolutely you are right! I just cannot imagine how horrible the situation would have been if you have forgotten everything!" Purnima hugged him strongly and made perfunctory kisses on his both cheeks. "But we must go to a psychiatrist as fast as possible. You have to recover all your memory as soon as possible. I am not thinking that it is a wise thing that you depend on Susmitha too much for anything."

"Why you are thinking like that?" Sameera asked her. As per what Pramod has said, Purnima has no objection for the friendship between them both.

"I am always has a hunch that Susmitha has got interest on you and trying to take you into her hold. Even she is aged thirty years or so, she is beautiful and youthful. Your too much dependency on her may lead to anything." suddenly there was fearful expression in the face of Purnima.

"This is the very first time you have expressed your fear in this way, is it is not?" Sameera understood Purnima never before expressed her fear like this to Pramod. Otherwise he would not have said like that to her. "But that Susmitha is a married woman and has a seven years aged daughter also."

"Of course, it is the first time that I am expressing my fear like this Pramod." Purnima sighed heavily and said "But you don't know our women' eyes. They are like x-ray go deep and see what is lying in the heart and mind also. My strong assumption is she so much wants to have it with you."

'How absolutely right this woman is', remembering what Pramod has said Sameera thought. "But dear what is the necessity to me to go to another woman once a beautiful woman like you is available to me all the time? Just shed unnecessary fears and try to be happy."

While they both were hugging each other like that, Sameera's fully erected penis was pressing onto Purnima's right thigh and there was a strong desire in her to fuck Purnima then and there.

"Until you have been cured absolutely I cannot be happy. One of the friends of my uncle is a reputed psychiatrist.........." she tried to say something.

"We sure do go to a psychiatrist but first finish this thing." Hugging her more strongly and kissing feverishly all over her face Sameera said with urgency.

"If you have forgotten about this also along with those things, I would have been quite peaceful now." She said with a sort of reluctance in her voice but started reciprocating with Sameera.

Sameera understood what Pramod said was absolutely true! There was pleasure in every fibre of her being while enjoying the body of Purnima with a male body. She tried to make Purnima absolutely naked but there came an angry expression into the face of Purnima. "Never, never I allow you to see me like that."

Sameera did not feel much anger or surprise on her reaction like that. She was even more conservative when it came to sex with her husband. Anyhow it was so much delicious to have a woman with a man body. Forgetting about the desire to make her completely nude, Sameera took away every cloth from her body and became absolutely nude. While she was doing that Purnima closed her face with both of her palms.

Sameera did not bother about her and started observing her own nude body which was Pramod's. It was with muscles and sportive! The thrill feeling in her heart has reached its motto when she found the erected penis with furious red tip! It was very much thrilling to her how it would be when she put it into the thing of Purnima.

"Enough looking at that bastard! If you finish it fast, there are other works that I have to attend." With an angry expression in her face Purnima said. By then Purnima opened her eyes and was looking at Sameera

Sameera also has no mood to argue with her as she was so much desired to have that taste as fast as possible. She put the petticoat of Purnima upto her thighs, made them astride and settled in between them before trying to put her right hand straight on her main thing.

"No," Closing her thighs near Purnima said with a firm voice. "I ever allowed you to do it like that?"

So all the women do think in the same way, Sameera thought in herself. She also never allowed her husband to have even a look at that. He has to struggle himself blindly to put his thing into hers. She also may have to do the same thing here. Thinking like that she occupied the body of Purnima and then Purnima widened her thighs to the maximum making it convenient to Sameera to place his thing at her main thing.

"I know that you cannot do it without my help." Before Sameera understood what was taking place her fully erected thing felt the fingers of Purnima around it and it was directed into something.

"Oh, my god! My god! How nice! How nice!" Sameera thought while her fully erected thing was sinking slowly between the tightly closed vaginal lips of Purnima. For the first time she was enjoying the pleasure in fucking rather than being fucked! The pleasure in fucking and being fucked may be equal but as it was completely new to her and as she cherished to have it for a long time, she was enjoying it to the maximum!

"Move your hips and discharge yourself into me fast." With little irritation in her face Purnima said. "I said to you I have lot of work to do now."

"Cannot you enjoy this for few minutes forgetting about all that work?" with a sort of irritation in her face, Sameera asked her.

"Sure I can. But now is not the time for it." she hugged Sameera tightly and kissed on her right cheek. "Be a good boy and fuck me fast. In the night we both do have it in the way you want with some exceptions."

What are those exceptions Sameera could understand without being told. Purnima never let her husband to look at her completely nude and do all the things he wanted.

"You never forget about those exceptions, ever you?" moving her hips furiously on the top of her, Sameera said angrily.

But the feeling was so great, so great! The joy was like this while a man moves his penis between the lips of a vagina! The lukewarm touch of the flesh of the vagina around the penis was wonderful and delicious! She just did not know to whom to be thankful for that great opportunity. She did not know how much of time has passed! While she was thinking like that and moving the penis, she suddenly released into her. The pleasure reached its motto while the grand release but immediately afterwards she felt as if she was drained off all her strength. She slumped herself just like an emptied sack on the top of Purnima.

"Relax, relax my dear! You are as much furious as every time! But you could not overcome your problem this time also." kissing on his forehead Purnima said and slowly made him to slide on his right side. "Now is the time to me to put myself into work." She got off from the bed.

"I have a problem? What is that problem?" with confusion in her face Sameera asked her.

"You cannot release yourself fast, that is your problem." Purnima laughed. "Most women may think such a problem to a man is a boon to them but I am not."

Then Sameera understood why she has not released even with the touch of Purnima's hand around that thing! She did not know whether to feel happy or sorrow for it. How Pramod was feeling about it?

"There is something else I want to say to you." Observing her minutely while she was adjusting her dress, Sameera said.

"Why don't you tell me all the things at one time?" by then she finished adjusting her dress and looked angrily into Sameera's face.

"I am sorry I forgot. If you come and sit beside me, I tell you what it is." Sameera sat straight on the bed without bothering to dress herself up. There was a sort of joy in her in being naked like that with the naked body of a man.

"I know your ploy. You do have me again if I come near to you." Purnima laughed and said. "Your thing is getting up again and I can see it."

"I promise I have no such idea." Pulling a serious expression into her face Sameera said. "And what I am going to say to you also is important."

"Alright, but if you try to do any mischief the deal for the night is off." Purnima said, came near to the bed and slumped beside him. "Now tell me what it is?"

"In the returning journey, I met one of my friends Sameera and we both sat side by side in the bus and talked. You need not develop any unnecessary doubts as she is just a friend to me and nothing more.

Moreover she has got married also." Looking into the face of Purnima with an uneasy expression, Sameera said.

"I never do develop any unnecessary doubts as I have absolute faith on you." Sighing heavily Purnima said. "Now tell me what it has to do anything with you?"

"After waking up she said to me that she also started feeling some memory problem. She also has no idea why it was so to her."

"I just cannot understand!" Purnima knitted her brows together. "Why she also has to face the same problem?"

"Just like me she too has no idea why it has happened like that to her."

"How much better you both know about each other?"

"Till we met in the bus, only to a little extent. Even less to friendship. We studied in the degree college together and just know the skeleton details of each other. But after meeting in the bus, we shared many a thing together."

"Did she say that she has any problem with her memory in her past life?" Purnima's knitted brows were kept like that.

"I did not ask her particularly about that."

"Now I ask you the same question. Did you have any psychological problems in your past?"

"I am perfect physically and psychologically. I never faced any such problem."

"Alright. I just don't know how to understand any of this." Purnima released her brows. "Don't worry I do believe you hundred percent." She smiled but with an uneasy expression in her face.

"Thank god! I really felt very much worried thinking that you never do believe what I said." There was relief in the face of Sameera.

"I know your character. I know what type of a person you are." With a fixed expression in her face Purnima said but once again frowns gathered in her face. "Have you got her phone number with you?"

"Of course, I got it. We have exchanged our phone numbers while we were parting."

"Then ask her how she is doing now. I am thinking as you both have got the same problem, at the same place and at the same time, the reason for it also the same for you both. Keeping tabs on what she is doing and how she is feeling also may be helpful to us."

"You are absolutely right. I talk with her." Sameera got off from the bed. "Now I have to go to the bank and see how the things are there. Once I finished with it, I talk with her."

"But you promised that you don't go to the bank the whole of this day." Once again Purnima knitted her brows. "Have you forgotten about it?"

"I promised like that but I am thinking now that it is better to go to the bank and see how the things are there. I am sorry, that I have to break that promise." With a sorrowful expression in her face Sameera said.

"But Pramod, are you sure that you can manage in the bank? You have forgotten even where is the bathroom in our house!" Once again there was anxiousness with gathered frowns in Purnima's face.

"You just don't worry. I take the help of Susmitha and you need not feel any fear about her. She is a very nice lady and she never has any intention like that."

After saying that with a smile on her lips and with an assured expression in her face, Sameera came out of the house after kissing Purnima on both her cheeks. But she phoned to Pramod and told him everything and advised him what better he would do in before itself rather than after her finishing the job in the bank.

x x x

Sameera did very nicely by saying like that, Pramod in the body of Sameera thought, saying like that would make the situation for him also easy and convenient. Anurag went to the office and his son was still sleeping by the time Sameera's phone came and Pramod felt very much happy on hearing her. After finishing talking with her, Pramod remembered that he did not take a bath yet. He went to the cupboard there, opened it and found Sameera's several dresses in it. There were several sarees also but he did not know how to wear a saree, so he selected a Punjabi dress from that and went into the bathroom.

That bathroom was a big and spacious one, clean and neat reflecting the richness of Anurag just like the other places in that big house. There was a big size mirror also in that bathroom, Pramod went and stood before it. Sameera was so beautiful indeed! Even with the dishevelled hair, rumpled clothes her body was appearing marvellous! He has to see it would be just like that until Sameera entered into it again.

But when that was going to happen? He was seeing the frowns gathered on the beautiful forehead of Sameera. Even he was feeling thrilling and happy to be in the beautiful body of Sameera, in an opposite sex which he was so much desired, the idea how long he has to stay like that was making him feel anxiousness. What if he has to remain in this body itself forever? That thought itself was very much horrifying but he understood one thing! There was no use in breaking head like that. He just has to wait until that soul transferring would happen again and till that moment enjoy himself with his strongly cherished desire all the time.

He sighed heavily and started taking the clothes one after one from Sameera's body. He was feeling mesmerised as marble like body of Sameera was being revealed to him little by little. When her both milky breasts were freed up from the brassiere also, they jumped up to their full length and he crossed his hands and took them both into his hands. The touch of them was smooth and silky but he was not feeling thrill in touching them in the body in which he was then.

Then he unknotted the petticoat and let it dropped at his feet, as Sameera did not wear anything inside her, nudeness of her under-parts completely came into his view. He stepped out of the petticoat and considered that public part. It seemed that Sameera shaved that part just two days or so back and there was little black stubble there. His wife Purnima never let him have a full look at her public part and on the few occasions when he managed to look at that part, he found dense black growth of hair there and it was indeed difficult to find her main thing under that growth. Even with hair also Pramod always interested to look at that place but Purnima never allowed him to do that.

With lot of thinking in himself, Pramod finished his bathing with shampoo and soap feeling lot of thrill while dealing with a female body like that.

x x x

"How was everything with you dear? Have you enjoyed your stay at your parents and the journey also? Is that alliance settled for your sister, will she marry that man?" in the night, when they both were on the bed together, taking Pramod near to him and kissing on his lips, Anurag asked.

'Oh, it is indeed nice, wonderful, marvellous!' Pramod thought. For the first time he understood how it would be to a woman in the hug of a male person, that too with a handsome guy like Anurag! He came to know how the reaction of a woman to that and he closed his eyes and crooned even more into Anurag's body while enjoying it a lot.

"You did not answer my question. There is lot of furore in your family about that issue. That boy not belongs to your caste and your family is quite against it. I think by now all you people have arrived at a solution and I want to know what it is?"

Pramod startled on hearing that! Sameera did not say anything about that and what he would say now? Now without any delay he has to say to him also what Sameera said to Purnima. In fact Pramod wanted to say that to Anurag later, after having that wonderful experience with him but there was no chance now. Unless he said so to him immediately now, Anurag would become lot of confused and got doubts also.

"I have to tell you a very important thing!" making himself distanced from him, Pramod said. "But I am feeling fear whether you do believe it or not."

"There is no question of my doubting with whatever you would say." With an encouraging smile on his lips Anurag said. "Just tell me what it is with an open heart."

"While returning from my parents' home, during the journey, I have got memory problem." With gathered frowns Sameera said. "I just don't know how it has happened. But now I am not able to remember certain things of my past and life."

"It is very much confusing! How something like that could happen?" Anurag knitted his brows together.

"I don't have even a vaguest idea why it has happened like that! I fell asleep in the bus and slept considerable period of time and I did not have even dreams also during that sleep. But when I woke up, I got this problem. However much hard I try, I just cannot remember certain things!"

"Thank god! You did not forget me and our son also." With relief in his face Anurag said.

"That is what my exact thinking also." Sameera said.

"But dear.........." once again frowns gathered on the forehead of Anurag. "...............how something like that could take place? Anything surprising, out of the place to the natural took place before the journey or after the journey?"

"Nothing like that." Nodding her head in negation Sameera said. "But one other surprising, coincident took place."

"May I know what it is?" Anurag's face was filled with a curious expression.

"In the bus I met a guy named Pramod. We were not very much close friends but studied in the college and knew each other. In the bus we sat side by side and shared about our lives and discussed many a thing. I think both of them slipped into sleep at the same time but by the time we both woke up, not only I but he also started facing the same memory problem. He also could not remember certain things of his past however much he tried."

"What? You both have been subjected to a similar problem at the same place and at the same time!" Anurag sat on the bed straight.

"It is absolutely like that." Sameera nodded her head. "He also felt happy as he did not forget about everything of his life. If we have forgotten about everything of our lives, we would have to wander on the road just like abandoned puppies."

"You are absolutely right dear!" with the same anxious expression in his face Anurag said. "I once again thank god that it has not happened like that."

"My sister's marriage is one of those things I cannot remember at all! When I forced myself to remember, I am feeling terrible headache." Pretending a painful expression in his face, Pramod said.

"Don't do any such type of a thing. As long as you can see our son and my family in a proper way, there is no problem even you don't remember certain things."

"Thank you, thank you very much!" what Anurag said then indeed relieved Pramod a lot, he immediately sat up on the bed, put his both hands around Anurag's neck and kissed on his both cheeks perfunctorily. "You are impeccably good."

"There is no necessity at all to praise me. Anyhow what's your wrong in whatever has taken place? Just feel relaxed and there is no problem whenever your memory sets alright." With the same assurance and even more happiness in his face, Anurag said. It appeared to Pramod that these types of hugs and kisses in the hands of Sameera were not usual him.

"I thought you would irritate on me after hearing about my problem like this. All husbands are not like you." Pramod said sighing heavily.

"If all the wives are like you, all the husbands are also would be just like me. Have you forgotten even that also how you used to be with our son? You love him and like him as if he is your own son. You promised to me that you do look after him in the same way all the time."

"It appears just like that." Pramod nodded his head. "I do keep the promise I made to you even I don't remember it now."

"Thank you dear!" he kissed on her lips straight and made her lay on the bed.

"How we both were used to be in sex?" when they both were laid fully on the bed parallel and facing each other, Pramod asked him.

"Alright, natural and in a nice way." Anurag laughed. "I don't feel surprise that you have forgotten about it also."

"Did I allow you to do everything you want to do with my body? I just want to know what type of sex we have been having." Thinking what type of things he always wanted to do with his wife, Pramod asked him.

"Sex is alright between us both always. You never denied me from having it whenever I wanted." He paused for a second and sighed heavily. "But it is always in the way you want it. We do have it only in a conservative and reserved way."

"But it is not going to be like that from now on." Pramod said with a smile. "You can have me in every way you want and there will be no restrictions at all. And it is another promise to you from me that it will be just like that for all the time to come."

"Really, really it will be like that?" Anurag's face was lit with lot of pleasure.

"It will be just like that and nothing else! Not just that, I do everything you want on your body also. I want sex between us should be in a full-fledged and hardcore way!"

"My god! I just cannot believe! How a radical change like this in you has become possible?" with a pleasant shocking expression in his face, Anurag asked him.

"I cannot say. But once I woke up from that sleep, I started feeling a terrible sexual urge and wanted to have it just like that. Moreover........." she paused for a second as if to reiterate whatever she was going to say. "............good husbands like you deserve to have their wives in their way they want."

"It is all quite unbelievable and shocking to me but in a very good way!" with the same happy expression in his face, Anurag said.

"Then put yourself into action and satisfy every kink of you with me in the way you want. There shall be no restrictions and no conservative approach." Pramod said with a smile on his lips.

Then Pramod remained just staring while Anurag started doing things. First he made himself absolutely naked. While he was taking clothes away from his body, Pramod observed him with a sort of interest. Even he was a man and it was not new to him, Pramod felt thrilled when Anurag's fully erected penis jumped free. It was as much big as Pramod's, furious with the red tip on the top of it. Just like his wife, Anurag also would have the habit of shaving his genitals and there was no hair at all on that. But like his wife Purnima, Pramod has no habit of shaving at that place and there was always abundant growth of black hair at his genitals.

The real action of him has taken place after he made Pramod absolutely nude and during that Pramod did not obstruct him even a little. While Anurag was enjoying each and every organ of Sameera's youthful body in a systematic way, Pramod understood how the sex with a male guy to the woman would be. He understood how the touch of a man on the breasts of a woman and while Pramod was sucking gently on the right breast of the Sameera's body and teasing the left nipple of her body with his left hand fingers, it was just pleasure,

pleasure and pleasure all the time to Pramod. By not allowing it in this way, Sameera has been losing a lot in her life.

"Do you know, it is the very first time that you let me deal with your breasts in this way." With lot of gratitude in his voice and a happy expression in his face, Pramod said looking into the face of Pramod.

"My poor husband! Why do you waste time? Just go on with what you are doing." Then Pramod took Anurag's ears-stubs into his both hands fingers at the same time and started teasing on them. This was something without his asking his wife would do which would give him sort of pleasure and kindle his desire to the maximum. It appeared it has had the same effect on Anurag also as Pramod has seen the change of expression in his face. Before Pramod has observed that expression a little more, Anurag took the other breast of Sameera's body and started sucking on it while teasing the right breast with his right hand fingers.

When he finished doing that and started trying to move down on Sameera's body, Pramod said "just a moment" and downed himself upto his chest.

"My god! It is indeed wonderful! Better than real fucking!" While Pramod circling the tip of his tongue around his right nipple while teasing the left nipple with his fingers, Anurag said with closed eyes while the unbearable pleasure was being expressed in his face. "But I am afraid I would burst before putting my thing into you."

"Don't worry. I help you to make it up." Just in few seconds it had happened like that and Pramod saw silvery drops gushing out from Anurag's erected thing. But with the touch of Sameera's body hands, just in seconds Anurag's penis bulged full.

"Beautiful! You are absolutely beautiful!" observing the naked body of Sameera on the bed Anurag said. "It is very first time that I am looking at an absolutely naked woman."

Sameera body's both the thighs were astride and even Pramod was a man in fact in the body of Sameera, he suddenly felt shame and tried to close the thighs.

"Please leave them like that. You promised me to let me enjoy you in the way I want." Still looking at the thing between the thighs minutely, Anurag said.

Pramod was feeling surprise that he was feeling shame like that! He never felt shame to become absolutely naked before his wife. But once his soul entered into a woman's body how he was feeling like that he could not understand! It appeared that the womanly characteristics were remained with the body even the soul entered into a male body. As he could not bear the shame at all, Pramod closed his face with both of his hands.

Suddenly there was a touch feeling between the thighs to Pramod and he felt a pleasure wave swept strongly all through his body and he understood it was the hand of Anurag. Pramod's heart was filled with immense pleasure while he was feeling the fingers of Anurag on the vagina and he could even sense a small gap was being made between the vaginal lips. When he sensed something bulged filled that gap, without being told he could understand what was happening! He has seen the fully bulged penis of Anurag and he was feeling fit and tight while it was moving between the tightly closed lips of the vagina and his whole body was filled with unbearable pleasure! He just hugged Anurag with both of his hands and kissed all over his face feverishly when he put his thing completely into Sameera's body and occupied it.

Then it has come into full knowledge of Pramod how it was being fucked rather than fucking! The pleasure was unbearable, immense and completely different while Anurag's bulged penis was moving between the tightly closed lips of Sameera body's vagina. He lost all the sense of time and just immersed himself in that sea of pleasure all the time keeping his hold gently around Anurag and really did not know how much of time passed but suddenly came into this world with the forceful thumps of Anurag and instantly felt the tremendous shivering of his thing deep inside him.

"I am just going to ask you to release yourself. You fucked me enough and I reached my orgasm." Kissing on Anurag's right cheek while putting his right hand fingers into his hair, Pramod said. "But just stay yourself like this. I want you top on my body for some more seconds."

Then Pramod understood why his wife used to ask him to stay like that even after releasing himself into her. There was joy in keeping his body like that even after he and herself also satisfied themselves.

"Thank you very much dear! Thank you! You just don't know how much I have enjoyed on this day. I must say it is just wonderful!" kissing on' the lips straight, Anurag said.

"You are going to enjoy yourself just like this every day from now on." Making him slide on the right side of him Pramod said.

"In the morning itself that gentleman Pramod called me. He asked me how I am doing? I said to him that there is no change in me and still I am feeling the same difficulty in remembering some things." Pramod said turning towards Anurag and putting his right hand around his neck.

"Pramod means that gentleman who travelled along with you in the bus?" Anurag knitted his brows.

"Yes, that gentleman who travelled along with me in the bus and has been facing a memory problem just like me now." Nodding his head Pramod said. "He said that his wife is planning to take him to a psychiatrist. One of the friends of her uncle is a reputed psychiatrist."

"Then dear why don't you also go and see that psychiatrist? You also have been facing a problem and need treatment." Anurag also put his hand around Pramod.

"Alright then. But why that psychiatrist only? There are so many psychiatrists around and you can take me to someone else."

"No dear" Anurag sat straight on the bed. "You both have faced the same problem, at the same time, at the same place. I am thinking that the reason also is the same for it. It is quite better that you do both see the same psychiatrist."

Pramod clipped his lower lip between his teeth frames for some time and said after releasing it slowly. "Alright. I talk to him."

"How far his house from here?"

"Ten or fifteen kilometres. Easily manageable in our car."

"While you are talking with him, tell him that we both come to his house. I want to see him also and talk with him."

"Good idea!" Pramod kissed on the lips of Anurag. "As you are making me to see the same psychiatrist he is going to see, it is indeed necessary that you see him and talk with him."

After talking some more time in themselves, they both did not know when they fell asleep.

x x x

"For the first time I am hearing something like this!"

Sameera was looking straight into the face of Susmitha who exclaimed like that after hearing the false story from Sameera which she told to Purnima also. Just like Purnima, Susmitha also was feeling very much surprise! She was absent to the bank on the previous day Sameera went and only the next day Sameera could meet her. Sameera immediately came back to the house on that day when she came to know that Susmitha was absent. The next day, Sameera called her into the cabin and started explaining everything to her which she said to Purnima and by the time she finished Susmitha was also just like Purnima surprised to the maximum.

"Are you sure that you have not hit hard your head with anything during your sleep? Most probably with the front seat. Without anything like that how this partial memory loss happens to you?"

"I am hundred percent sure that I have not hit my head with anything like that during that sleep or any other time." With little irritation in her voice Sameera said. "Have you forgotten what I have said? It was not just I who suffered with such a problem. That girl also has been suffering like that just in the same way from that moment."

"I just.............I just..............cannot understand! How both people at the same time, same place face the same problem?" Susmitha knitted her brows together.

"You need not break your head to know about that as I have been doing only that from the moment it occurred." Sighing heavily Sameera said. "What all you have to do is; you have to help me with everything in the bank until I completely recover my memory. Many a thing I just cannot remember now."

"Do you need to ask me like this?" Sameera felt just like current passed through the body when Susmitha took her right hand into her hands and squeezed it gently. It was the first time or in before also Susmitha clutched Pramod's hand like that Sameera did not know. Even her soul was a woman how she was feeling thrill like that by the touch of a woman just because she was in a male body, she could not understand. It was just like that even the soul left the body; all the male characteristics left with the body itself. "I not only help you to do the work in the bank but in recovering your memory also."

Sameera slowly relieved her hand from the hands of Susmitha and put herself into thinking. There was no surprise in Purnima's feeling fear. Even more aged than Purnima, Susmitha was more beautiful! It was indeed difficult to think that she was a mother of a seven years aged daughter.

"Thank you very much!" with full gratitude in her face and voice Sameera said.

"Don't dare to thank me at all!" with an angry expression in her face Susmitha said. "If you are feeling too much grateful for what I am going to do, you just do one thing."

"Tell me what it is?" Sameera started feeling fear thinking what she was going to ask.

"Come and have tea in my home in the evening."

"Such a simple thing! Really I do love it." Sameera laughed still feeling uneasily.

x x x

On the evening of that day, Sameera went to the house of Susmitha in Susmitha's car. But by the time they both reached the house of Susmitha, her husband Pallav and daughter Renuka were moving out. By the way of their both greeting her, Sameera understood that Pramod was quite known to them both.

"After a long time I took my friend to our home and you both are going away?" Susmitha angrily asked looking into the faces of her daughter and husband.

"I am really very sorry. But I have promised to our daughter to take her to a movie. If I don't take her now, she eats me away." With a sorrowful expression in his face Pallav said.

Renuka, Susmitha's daughter was beautiful just like her mother but Pallav was a lean personality with five feet height. There was no surprise at all if he did not have much sexual libido.

"Never mind. You both go and enjoy for the present. I come to your home again to spend time with you both."

After that Pallav and Renuka moved away from that place. Before moving away from there, Pallav looked into the faces of Sameera and Susmitha with a sort of expression which Sameera felt very much odd.

"You have got a beautiful family! Cute daughter and nice husband! You ought to be very much happy." Sipping the coffee which Susmitha gave to her while adjusting herself for more comfort in the chair she sat, Sameera said.

"This itself proves that you have forgotten certain important things!" Susmitha slumped in the chair opposite to Sameera with a coffee cup in her hand. "But I have no objection to refresh your memory."

Sameera did not ask feeling fear what Susmitha would say if she asked. But it appeared that Susmitha was going to tell even she was not asked about that.

"I really don't mind Pallav's doing a name sake job. The money I have been getting through my job is enough for all our purposes. But I already told you, shedding all my shame,.........." she paused for a second and closed her eyes as if she could not look into the face of Sameera. "I just cannot understand how he has given me such a beautiful baby! Everything happens just in seconds. When he puts it in and when takes it out only he knows. A long time back only on one occasion he could manage to keep it there until releasing the seeds so the result was Renuka."

'My god! What I am hearing!'Sameera's heart beat increased! She should not have come to this place at all. But she could not deny that making Susmitha dissatisfied knowing how much of Susmitha's help she needed in future.

"I always think how it is having that thing fiercely moving up and down in my thing while my body has been crushing under the weight of a man! A man like you handsome and strongly built! I just don't know how much I have been craving for that."

Sameera's heart beat increased even more. She understood how painful it was without having it sufficient for a woman. For the first time she came to know it was not just men suffer with starvation of sex but women also.

"You may feel wonder why cannot I have it with someone and satisfy myself. Men are more than enough to give it if a woman like me asks them for it. But I just don't know why but I cannot have it with anyone else except you. I have the feeling and desire to have it with only you but with no one else. I even forsake my promotion as a manager and remained in the bank to have that with you. But you are so cruel Pramod, you never do consider about my wish."

Sameera's heart was filled with shock! That scoundrel Pramod did not tell her that this thing was this much deep. She did not know what to say.

"You don't feel fear Pramod. I never force you to have it with me unless you come yourself to me for that. But when you do that........." suddenly there was a serious expression in her face. "..............don't forget that you are doing a great favour to me."

"What your husband thinks if ever he comes to know that you are thinking like this?" with full uneasiness in her heart Sameera asked her.

"Long before he acknowledged his weakness and my absolute dissatisfaction because of his weakness. He told me many a time that he has no objection if I satisfy my urge with anyone if I want. He knows that I have a strong feeling on you and he provides an amicable opportunity to both of us to have it together. In fact when I phoned to him that I was coming to home along with you, he planned himself to go out with our daughter only to facilitate it to us both."

"I just don't know what to talk and what to say." With complete confusion and shock in her face Sameera said. "I don't remember any of this even a little bit."

"Then you forget about everything what I said." Leaning back in the chair Susmitha said. "My cooperation in the bank to you will be as I promised. You need not doubt it even a little bit."

"Alright then. May I go home now?" Sameera got off from the chair she sat. "Purnima may be waiting for me in the home."

Susmitha nodded her head and she also got off from the chair she sat. But feeling the same uneasiness and discomfort in her heart Sameera came to Pramod's house.

x x x

"My friend is a reputed psychiatrist of course. But he believes in paranormal also which I don't like at all." Purnima's uncle Ratnarao said. The problem has been explained clearly to Ratnarao by Purnima and she said about Pramod and Sameera both the issues all clearly basing on whatever she heard from Sameera.

As promised to Anurag, Pramod phoned to Sameera and told her that he also wanted to see the same psychiatrist that Sameera was going to see and said to her that Anurag wanted to see her also. Then the next day morning itself Anurag and Pramod came to the house of Pramod and talked with Sameera and Purnima. On that evening itself all of them went to the house of Purnima's uncle Ratnarao whose friend was the reputed psychiatrist.

"Such a paranormal thing has taken place in our lives. As such I am thinking that it is better to see a psychiatrist who believes in paranormal also." Sameera said.

"Then its okay. I secure an appointment with him. Then you both go and see him and tell him the problems you are facing. I am hundred percent sure that he will certainly be helpful to you people." Ratnarao said.

"Is it is not possible to go straight and see him?" Anurag asked him.

"He is a very busy psychiatrist and seeing him without an appointment is not possible. I try to secure an appointment to you both with him as soon as possible and let you know." Ratnarao promised to him.

After spending sometime with that Ratnarao, all of them went to their respective homes.

x x x

"As you both have subjected to the same problem at the same time and at the same place, I am thinking that it is better that I do see of you both at a single time. Ratnarao very clearly told me about you both and your problem along with your names."

As promised Ratnarao managed appointment of the psychiatrist Manohara Rao on the next day evening itself. Pramod, Purnima, Anurag and Sameera went to him at that appointed time.

Pramod and Sameera looked into each other's faces with happy expressions. "We have no objection to that doctor." Pramod said and Sameera also nodded her head in agreement.

"May I also present with them doctor?" Anurag asked.

"First I talk only with the patients and then I allow the relatives also with them. After having full discussion with these two, I discuss about it with you both also. First I have to ascertain what is the reason for this phenomena." Manohara Rao said.

Anurag and Purnima looked into each other's faces and nodded their heads with uneasy expressions.

"You both go outside and sit in the chairs there. I call you both inside when I finish with these both."

With the same uneasy expressions in their faces, Anurag and Purnima came out of that chamber.

x x x

"Partial memory loss is not that much of a surprising thing and sometimes it happens to people. Happening it to you both who are young and healthy is of course surprising to me but happening it to you both at the same time and at the same place, I just cannot understand how it has become possible!" Once only they both were with him, Manohara Rao said looking into the faces of Pramod and Sameera.

"Sir, do you believe in paranormal?" Sameera asked him as if she did not hear what he has said.

"Of course, I do believe in paranormal. That is why more people do like to call me as a parapsychologist rather than psychiatrist." Manohara Rao laughed. "But I don't believe in every little unbelievable thing as paranormal. Anyhow why did you ask me like that?"

"What happened to us is not at all partial memory loss. It is entirely different!"

"I just cannot understand what do you want to tell me!" with a confusing expression in his face Manohara Rao said.

"I am thinking that it is better to tell him the entire truth." Looking into the face of Pramod, Sameera said.

"If you are thinking that is the best thing to do, I have no objection whatsoever." Pramod said.

"Sir, I do start at the beginning and I cannot say whether there is any paranormal involved in it or not but whatever has taken place is quite unbelievable to ourselves. Just listen to me." Then she told him everything; how they both met in the bus, how they shared about their lives with each other and how strongly they wished to be the opposite sex and shared that also with the each other. "Just before slipping into sleep, I thought how nice it would have been if I become Pramod who is handsome and young to experience everything that an opposite sex enjoys." Sameera sighed heavily after saying that also and it took nearly half an hour to her to explain that so to that psychiatrist.

"And I also thought it would be just wonderful if I become Sameera as I can have the perfect feeling of opposite sex with a beautiful body and after that I fell into sleep." Pramod said.

"But when we woke up, we found ourselves in the other body! That means I started feeling in the body of Pramod and Pramod started feeling in my body. It is just like souls changed in our bodies." Sameera said.

"What? I just cannot understand what you are saying!" with a shocking expression in his face Manohara Rao said.

"We too cannot understand even a little bit but that was what exactly has taken place." Once again sighing heavily Sameera said.

"That means I am talking with Sameera not Pramod!" looking into the eyes of the body of Pramod, Manohara Rao said still with the same shock and surprise.

"You are absolutely right sir." With a smile on her lips Sameera said.

"And I am Pramod in the body of Sameera here." When Pramod said that Manohara Rao looked at the body of Sameera with the same unbelievable expression in his face. "As we ourselves cannot believe this, there is no surprise in your feeling shock like that."

"I heard about souls changing the bodies. But as per my knowledge there is a necessity of a dead body also. One person's soul has to empty his body by entering into the dead body and then only any other person's soul can enter into him. Here, without any dead body present there; your souls have changed places like that!"

"So you do believe in paranormal. You do believe in souls changing places." Pramod asked him.

"I did not see with my own eyes that thing but I do believe." Manohara Rao nodded his head. "I do believe of course that your souls have changed places like that. But I just don't know how I can be helpful to you both if that is the case."

On hearing that Sameera and Pramod exchanged anxious glances.

"Sir, if you yourself who has belief in paranormal say like that, I just don't where we can go." Pramod anxiously said. "We just don't know what to do and how long we have to continue like this in other person's body."

"Alright, I do try to help you." Nodding his head Manohara Rao said. "Before your souls changing the bodies like that, you both wish to be the opposite sex and want to see how that experience would be."

"Very much strongly sir, in fact that much strongly I even contemplated to become a transgender." Sameera said with a smile. "In fact I have been enjoying a lot to be in the body of opposite sex."

"The same is with me also sir. Even it is very much confusing, perplexing and disturbing to me, I also have been enjoying to be in the body of Sameera." Pramod said.

"Why this partial memory loss story then?" Manohara Rao knitted his brows together.

"We just cannot imagine how the spouses of us both do react if we say what exactly took place. And it is very difficult to convince the outside world about that. So presently we are managing ourselves like this." Pramod said.

"I must say you both are clever indeed!" laughing loudly Manohara Rao said

Pramod and Sameera also laughed on hearing that but suddenly with a serious expression in her face Sameera asked "But sir how long we have to be like this? When we can change into our respective bodies?"

"As per your present state you have been enjoying being in the opposite sex, is it is not so?"

"Yes, of course" Pramod said and both of them nodded their heads.

"You have not yet completely satisfied with your strong desire to be in the opposite sex."

Pramod and Sameera looked into each other's faces and this time Sameera answered. "That also is right."

"Then I am thinking............" Manohara Rao leaned back in the chair and said "...........unless you both have been completely satisfied with your respective desires, I don't think the changing of your souls into respective bodies take place."

"But sir I agree still we have not satisfied completely with our desires but we don't want to stay in the other's body like this." With an anxious expression in her face Sameera said.

"Changing of souls did not take place with your consent before. I am thinking it happens just like before, in future also. It is just my thinking that the changing of souls may take place after your desires are completely satisfied. Even I do believe in paranormal, this type of thing is completely new to me. I just cannot see how can I will be helpful to you in this regard."

Pramod and Sameera looked into each other's faces again with the same anxious expressions but they did not say anything.

"I am thinking that you both do spend time in close proximity as much as possible just like in the bus and at one time changing of souls may take place again and you can feel in your own body then. But my strong idea is unless you both have been satisfied with your strong odd desires, you may not have your own body."

"Really, really all this is very much perplexing and troubling to me. Still I cannot believe in any of this." Covering his face with both of his hands and leaning back in the chair, Pramod said.

"There is no use whatsoever by worrying yourselves like this." Manohara Rao stooped forward and balanced his both arms on the table in between. "You both just try to continue in the other body as you have been doing. Just enjoy all the time being in the opposite sex. Satisfying your odd desires to the maximum also is important for the souls change again. In the meantime I do search and try to know if ever any people have experienced changing of souls like this and any remedy is available to this."

"Thank you, thank you very much sir!" with a grateful expression in her face Sameera said.

"Now you both can go and enjoy your present state forgetting about the complexities of it." Manohara Rao leaned back in the chair "What should I tell you to your spouses' now?"

"Tell them it is indeed some partial memory loss and will be cured if all our desires have been satisfied without any reservation." Sameera said with a smile on her lips. "This Pramod's wife is indeed very conservative type. She is not letting me satisfy all my kinks as a man!"

"Just say the same thing to Anurag also but he is satisfying every desire of me without being asked." Pramod laughed and said "But if they say about any hypnotherapy etcetera tell them that they don't work out. You know now exactly what is the problem."

"You are right! Now is the time to talk with your spouses." Manaohar Rao said. "You both go out and send them in. Just remember! I am always available to you in phone and physically also to share your problems with me."

"Thank you very much sir." Sameera stood up from her chair and said and Pramod also said "Thank you." after vacating his chair.

xxx

"This partial memory loss happens due to unfulfilled strong desires also. You both try to know if there are any unfulfilled strong desires in your spouses and fulfil them. That helps them in recovering their memory full. Except this we cannot do anything in this regard now." Looking at both Purnima and Anurag, Manohara Rao said.

"But sir how it is if you try hypnotherapy or something like that on both of them?" Sameera asked with a dissatisfying expression in her face. This was not what she has expected to hear from that psychiatrist.

"Using hypnotherapy or any other psychiatric treatment now is dangerous! I cannot recommend that now. But I can suggest something to both you people for the present." Manohara Rao stooped forward and balanced his arms on the table in between while looking into the faces of both of them.

"Tell me sir, what it is?" Anurag also was feeling dissatisfaction with what Manohara Rao said but he did not show it in his face.

"They both have been suffered this partial memory loss when they both were together. The reason might be a single one for that. I am thinking that they both get their full memory at one point of time if they both try to spend time together as much as possible."

Anurag and Purnima looked into each other's faces and Purnima said before Anurag saying anything. "I have no objection to that. He has to get his full memory back as soon as possible." She did not like Pramod's depending too much on the assistant manager Susmitha. She has the strong feeling that Susmitha was trying to take her husband into her hold.

"I too have no objection." Anurag did not like much that Sameera spending time with Pramod but when Purnima said like that he did not know what else to say.

"Okay. You both can go now. But just remember. Two things are very much important now." Leaning back in the chair Manohara Rao paused for a second as if to reiterate whatever he was going to say. "Fulfilling all their desires and making them spend time together are very much important to make them recover their full memory."

"Alright sir." Purnima nodded her head and got off from the chair and Pramod also followed her suit.

x x x

"This psychiatrist is quite dissatisfying to me. I am thinking that we may better meet another psychiatrist in this regard." When the four settled in the house of Pramod, Purnima said with lot of irritation.

"I am also of the same opinion." Anurag said.

"But this psychiatrist is very reputed psychiatrist! You yourself said that." Sameera said.

"But what's the use if he does not give us the best solution to our problems." The irritation in Purnima was not lessened even a little.

"I am not thinking like that. He appeared very wise and understood the problem. I don't think that he would say anything without reason." Pramod said.

"I am also thinking in the same way." Sameera said.

Purnima was about to say something more but before that Anurag said. "Mrs. Purnima once these both are feeling good with that psychiatrist, we may better follow what he has said. If they don't feel any inconvenience with their memory problem why do we worry about it?"

'My position is not like your position.' Purnima was thinking irritatingly. 'It seems that Pramod has been enjoying depending on Susmitha a lot.' Putting her full effort not to show her inner feeling on her face, Purnima said "alright."

After discussing some more time in themselves, Anurag and Pramod left that place.

x x x

"It is still very much unbelievable to me! Even after this many days also I just cannot believe it took place like that!" Pramod said with a surprising expression in his face. "But I cannot say I am not enjoying this."

They both were out and talking with each other sitting in a park. Once it has been advised by the psychiatrist like that, Purnima and Anurag were forcing them to meet as often as possible and spend time together.

"I am also enjoying it to the maximum while feeling anxiousness when can I enter into my own body again." Sameera said. "I don't want to stay in your body forever even it is so much thrilling and enjoying to me."

"Don't forget you even considered to undergo transgender operation for enjoying this, were not you?" with a small smile on his lips Pramod said. "I am also enjoying of course but I am also feeling the same anxiousness. I too don't want to stay in your body forever and feeling worry ever it is possible that I go into my body again or not."

On hearing that Sameera's face also has become anxious. "No, that very idea is creating lot of anxiousness in me. I like and strongly wish to enjoy being an opposite sex and presently I am doing that and not satisfied completely yet. But I like and enjoy being a woman also. Moreover I just want to be in my body and I cannot even imagine losing it forever."

"One thing we both have to understand!" Pramod said. "Worrying ourselves like this is not going to solve our problem. As that psychiatrist said, even however much we wished to be the opposite sex, it did not take place with our consent and knowledge. Just in the same way our souls have to go into their respective bodies in an automatic way."

"And that is possible only after we completely satisfy ourselves the desire of being opposite sex! I am thinking that psychiatrist is absolutely correct in his logic! Unless we satisfy our desire to be in the opposite sex hundred percent, our souls transferring again may not be possible." With a meaningful expression in her face, Sameera said.

"Anurag is a nice guy! From the beginning I just could satisfy every desire of me to be in the opposite sex." Pramod laughed and said.

"It was not so with Purnima! She was so much conservative and reserved! But after hearing from the psychiatrist like that, she has been allowing me to have her almost in the way I want. There that psychiatrist did me a great help." Sameera laughed and said.

"But you also used to be very much conservative with Anurag I understood." Pramod angrily said. "I just cannot say how much happy he felt when I allowed him to do whatever he wanted with my body."

"Then you allowed him to satisfy all his kinks with you?" with gathered frowns and angry expression Sameera asked.

"Yes, of course!" nodding his head Pramod said. "Not just that, I promised to him that it would be just so to him forever in his life."

"Who you are to make a promise like that?" Sameera got off from the bench and yelled. "I can understand what type of desires he has! I just cannot bear if he is doing all that with me."

"Tell me one thing!" Pramod pulled a serious expression into his face. "Are not you feeling such kinks in you after entering into my body?"

"Yes, of course." Sameera nodded her head. "I have been satisfying them with your wife also now. But I just cannot bear if Anurag does all that with me. In fact I don't want to have sex in full-fledged way with him."

"But why?" the serious expression in Pramod's face was intensified even more. "So far I understood very well that you have not been living so intimately and happily with Anurag. I agree that he is considerably old to you. But he has very good mentality and has been helping your family also a lot. Then what's the problem to you to be in the way he wanted? To be his loving and caring wife?"

Sameera covered her face with both of her hands and leaned back in the chair.

"I must know the answer Sameera. In a most strange way both of our lives are interlinked like that. There must not be any secrets between us both. Tell me what is the reason? Why cannot you love your husband with whole of your heart?"

Still there was no answer from Sameera and she did not remove her hands from her face. It appeared that she was struggling very much to say anything about it to Pramod.

"There must not be any secrets between us. You have to tell me." With firmness Pramod said. "Just tell me what is the reason?"

"I am in love with someone else. We both wanted to marry and we have been having it together now also. Entering into the life of Anurag is out of compulsion! That is why I just cannot love him and have sex with him in a full-fledged way." Sameera removed her hands from her face and said but without looking into the face of Pramod.

"What's the bloody hell you are talking?" with a shocking expression in his face Pramod asked her. "I don't feel that much of surprise if you have been in love with someone before marrying Anurag. But I just cannot understand you have been having it with your lover now also."

"Yes, that's right!" Sameera looked into the face of Pramod and nodded her head. "That guy is living in the house next to us. Every time I do go to my home, I go to him also and have it with him. As he cannot forget me and is in love with me still, I cannot remain without loving him back and am having it with him also. That is why I cannot love Anurag wholeheartedly." Once again she covered her face with both of her hands and suddenly burst into weeping.

"Don't you know how much of big mistake you are committing? You have been cheating a very good husband like him. Your infidelity is inexcusable!" Pramod angrily yelled.

"I agree but I am helpless! That Vilok cannot forget me at all and remained unmarried! He just cannot digest and understand that I have become the wife of another man. I just cannot bear if he worries for anything. So I am helpless and continuing loving him like that." With a helpless expression in her face, Sameera said. "But if he forgets me and marry I can forget him and lead my life happily with Anurag."

"Is this matter known in your family also?" Pramod knitted his brows together.

"How they did not know about it? We have been lovers for a long time."

"Still they forced you to marry Anurag!"

"Yes, they did. I also have to agree because of the circumstances of our family was in then. But........" once again there came change in the voice of Sameera. "............ I am feeling very much guilty. Anurag is a very good guy and he is not only being a very good husband to me but helping my family also in many respects. I am cheating him by being infidel like that to him which I don't like at all." Once again she covered her face and burst into weeping.

"Did not you try to make your lover understand this point?"

"I have been trying all the time. But he is madly in love with me and not listening to me whatever I am saying. What should I do?" once again Sameera looked into the face of Pramod with the same helpless expression in her face. "In fact a girl named Latha who has been working with him in his office is so madly in love with him and wants to marry him. But because of his love on me, he is not agreeing to marry her."

"What his family members saying about it? How they have been allowing him to have such a relationship with you even after your marriage also." Surprise masked the face of Pramod.

"He is an orphan! He has been living all alone in that house."

"I cannot understand how your family members are allowing you to go to him now."

"I am very much persistent and they are helpless." Sameera sighed heavily. "They are with a guilty feeling as they made me married against my wish and allowing me to go to him."

There was some silence between them both until Pramod broke it. "Anurag asked about your family matters to me. He asked me about your sister's marriage with a guy with whom she is also in love with. All your family members have been opposing to her marriage as that guy belongs to other caste."

"Both of them have found a perfect solution to solve that problem." Sameera suddenly laughed. "With what option our family has been left with after my sister is pregnant with that guy and it came to be known to us only at the six month of it?"

"My god! Both your sisters are equal to each other." Once again with a shocking expression in his face Pramod said. "But your sister is better than you. She is marrying the person with whom she is in love with."

"Once I am so much against marrying Anurag, my family members tried to fix my sister's marriage with him. But my sister is not as much glamorous as I and Anurag wanted to marry only me. So it has happened like this." Sighing heavily Sameera said.

There was some silence between them both until it was broken by Sameera. "My sister's marriage is going to be performed just in one week and you have to go to there. I tell you every detail of my family to you and you have to be very careful."

"Sure I would be." Pramod nodded his head while some plan was forming in his mind. "And you also need to be very careful! Especially with that Susmitha. She has been seeing just for an opportunity to eat me away."

"I agree with that. But she has been helping me very much in managing the affairs in the bank." Sameera said. "We both have been talked a lot in her home. After hearing her in full, I felt lot of pity on her. Did not you ever feel like that?"

"I felt like that and still am feeling so. But what can I do?" knitting his brows together Pramod said. "I cannot cheat my wife and be infidel to her." There was sudden firmness in his voice.

"Shall we go to our respective homes then?" getting off from the place she sat Sameera said. "We talk indeed a lot by now. We fix a date mutually and meet again."

"Alright" Pramod also nodded his head and got off from the bench and said. Then they both retired from that place to their respective homes.

x x x

"Can we both take leave in this afternoon? Will there be any problem if we do it like that?" Sameera asked Susmitha.

"There will be no grave problem and it can be manageable." With a smile and surprise in her face Susmitha said. "But for what purpose?"

"I want to come to your home." Leaning back in the chair Sameera said. "Can you manage your husband and daughter also not present at home while we are in it?"

"Pallav returns from his office only at seven in the night and he took our daughter Renuka along with him from her tuition centre. I don't need to put any effort for that." A serious and meaningful expression came into the face of Susmitha. It was just like she understood what Sameera meant.

"Then we both go to your home in the afternoon and have our lunch also there." There was a fixed expression in her face and firmness in Sameera's voice.

Susmitha nodded her head with a smile on her lips.

x x x

"I never did even imagine that you do agree to this!" both of their naked bodies were side by side on the bed in Susmitha's bedroom and both of them have it in a full-fledged manner "How much I dreamt for it! How much I wanted it!" she exclaimed with an utmost pleasant expression in her face.

"Anyhow is it is upto your expectation or not?" the experience with Susmitha was so much enjoyable to Sameera also. She has satisfied even those kinks also with Susmitha which she could not satisfy with Purnima.

"You rascal! You are asking that question to me?" Susmitha kissed perfunctorily on both the cheeks of Sameera. "You just have killed me with pleasure! No guy with whom I have it did it with me like this!"

"That means you have this experience with guys other than Vilok also." With a smile on her lips Sameera asked her.

"I must say yes." Susmitha nodded her head in agreement. "I had it with one or two guys before Vilok entered into my life. But a sense of morality has entered into me and never could infidel to Vilok until now."

"Are you feeling bad that you have to cheat him now like this?" knitting her brows together Sameera asked her.

"Yes, there is a sort of guiltiness in me even though Vilok has given his permission to me for it." sighing heavily Susmitha said. "But my strong desire to have it with you dominated every other feeling. I want to have it with you as many times as possible."

"We do try to have it together as many times as possible. But I cannot say how long we both can work together in that bank."

"For the present we both don't worry about it. Anyhow if we really do want it, we can have it together occasionally wherever we may be." Sighing heavily Susmitha said. "But you have been quite against to this for a long time. What really made you to agree to this?"

"In fact for a long time I have been thinking about it also. Once you are feeling that much strongly for it only from me, ultimately I came to the opinion that it is wrong if I don't agree to it. But I must say one thing to you here.........." Sameera paused for a second as if to reiterate whatever she was going to say. ".........I also enjoyed it as much as you did and want to have it with you as often as possible."

That might have triggered something in Susmitha again and she once again hugged Sameera strongly and kissed all over Sameera's face feverishly. "You just don't how much happy I am feeling hearing this! For a long time I have been absolutely starving for it and your cooperation like this just satisfy my desire in full. In fact Vilok and I stopped having it together since long time back."

"I just cannot understand! Why it is so?" Sammera knitted her brows together.

"Vilok stopped feeling any sexual desire and he has become a eunuch almost." She sighed heavily and said.

"I really pity him as he cannot enjoy a beauty like you." Then Sameera also hugged Susmitha strongly and kissed on her lips straight.

Then they both of them have it together in a full-fledged manner again with the same sort of pleasure.

x x x

"Can you love me in the same way all the time whatever you come to know about me?" on that day after they have it in a full-fledged manner in the way Anurag liked it, Pramod asked him.

"My love on you never does change. Whatever I come to know about you; it just remains the same all the time." There was firmness in the voice of Anurag. "Anyhow why did you want to ask this question now?"

Pramod clipped his lower lip between his teeth frames and started chewing on it. He was feeling very much uneasy to tell that to him even however much he decided to do that.

"If you don't express to me freely everything, I think that you don't believe me at all." While looking straight into the face of Pramod, Anurag said.

Pramod released the lip, nodded his head as if he came to a decision and opened his mouth. "Before I have become your wife, I was in love with someone. In fact I have been forced to marry you because of my family circumstances at that time. We terribly need financial assistance and you can provide that to us if I marry you. So my marriage was with you."

"I am terribly sorry on hearing this." There was deep hurt feeling in the face of Anurag. "If I have been known about this, I never would have made you marry me."

"After marriage with me also, I just could not forget that guy and thought about him. So I could not behave all happy way with you. But recently a sudden transformation took in me. I have realised that I should love only my husband and no one else. So I transferred all my love from that guy onto you and can offer myself like this to you all the time." With the same genuine expression in his face Pramod said.

"I just don't know whether to feel happy or sorrow on hearing this." There was confusion and happy expression in the face of Anurag. "But I have suspected something like this from your behaviour. It is not at all a surprising thing that now a day girls are in love with someone before their marriage and marry someone else because of the circumstances."

"But I am not regretting for whatever has taken place. Marriages are the decision of god and we have to accept the spouse enter into our lives with whole of our hearts. That is what I am doing now." Sighing heavily Pramod said. "But we both have to do something now."

"Let me know what it is?" with a curious expression in his face Anurag asked. "I am always ready to do whatever you ask me to do."

"That guy who has been in love with me cannot forget me at all. We both have to make him forget me." Looking straight into the face of Anurag, Pramod said. "Yes, we both together have to do that. We have to make him forget me and agree to marry the girl Latha who has been in love with him a lot."

"I have no objection whatsoever to do that." With the same happy expression in his face Anurag said. "But when we both have to do it?"

"We both have to go to my parents' home just in two days for my sister's marriage. Then we need to do it."

"Alright then." Anurag said and nodded his head. "It seems that there is an improvement in your memory. You can recover those things which you could not before."

"A little of course." Sameera laughed and said. "If that Pramod and I spend time together for some more occasions, I think my memory problem will be solved completely."

"I have no objection whatsoever to it." Anurag said but he did not like much their spending together time. With effort he managed his inner feeling not expressed in his face.

x x x

"That's it Vilok. Now Anurag is my husband and I love him wholeheartedly. If your love on me is genuine and you really do love me, you have to forget your love on me."

Vilok indeed shocked when he saw Sameera and her husband also in his house. He was even more shocked when Sameera started talking and said what she really wanted.

"I really don't mind the love between you both before our marriage. But after marriage, I am not thinking it is that much proper that you still do love Sameera. If you cannot forget her at all, the only proper course is that you do marry her after our divorce." Anurag said.

"I never do agree to it. I am ready even to die myself but I don't agree to divorce you now and marry this guy." The firmness in Pramod's voice then surprised both Anurag and Vilok also.

"Please don't say like that." With shock and sorrowful expression in his face Vilok said. "Alright. If you don't like it at all, we do put a stop to it."

"Just that is not enough Vilok. You have to marry Latha also who has been so madly in love with you. Then only I can feel happy."

"As you said we put a stop to our love relationship forever however much difficult it is to me. Even it is so much painful to me, once your marriage was over with this guy that is the only proper thing, I agree. But........." with a distressing expression in his face, Vilok said. "..........don't force me to marry Latha. I cannot do that."

"If you really want my happiness, you have to do it. I never can feel happy if you remain like this." Sameera said without losing the firmness in her voice. "You must do that also."

"Then only I can believe what you have said. If you remain unmarried like this, I have to think you are still in love with my wife." Anurag said.

"Alright. As you said." Vilok nodded his head with a painful expression in his face after seriously pondering over that matter for few seconds.

x x x

"I must say you did a marvellous thing!" after hearing everything from Pramod, Sameera said with a happy expression in her face. "I just don't know how to solve that problem! You have even made him married that girl!"

"Yes, I did it." relieving from Sameera's hold gently Pramod said. "From now on you can spend loving and happy life with Anurag."

Once again Pramod and Sameera met in that park and started talking.

"That happens only when I enter into my body again. Until that moment, it is only you who are going to lead loving and happy life with Anurag." Sameera laughed and her face suddenly became serious. "I need to tell you some important thing here."

"I am very much eager to hear that!" Pramod said looking curiously into the face of Sameera.

When Sameera said about him that she and Susmitha have it together, Pramod first shocked and then exploded with anger. "Why the hell you did such type of a thing, such infidelity to my wife?"

"I just could not see her suffering like that. So, we both have it together." Sighing heavily Sameera said. "Not just that; we have been having it together and I promised to her that we can have it so as many times as possible."

"You.......you.......I just don't know what to do to you. I just cannot bear my anger." Pramod angrily yelled.

"You did a lot affecting my life. But for a simple thing I did out of sympathy you are becoming like this." Sameera irritatingly said.

"Whatever I did, I did for good. I have prevented immorality from being continued and give yourself to your husband like that is just your duty. But what you did in my place? You paved way for immorality."

"I just could not think like that. She is starving for sex and suffering like that! Moreover after having help from her like that in the bank, I thought it was just my duty." Sameera sighed heavily. "If you want me to behave in the way you are doing with my husband now, you need to continue that with Susmitha. There is no other way."

"No, that is never possible." Pramod angrily yelled.

"Then behaving in that amicable way with Anurag also is not possible." Sameera said with firmness.

The meeting was abruptly broken then and they both went to their respective places angrily.

x x x

After that day, the anger in them was gradually subsided, they understood the situation and Sameera and Pramod were meeting each other not only in that park but in other places also. So far they completely satisfied their desire to be in the opposite sex and so desperately wanted to be in their own body. They met and talk with the Manohara Rao also and told him that too that their desire to be the opposite sex was completely satisfied. He said to them to spend time together as much time as possible as that only can facilitate the souls' transferring again. They have been meeting as many times as possible and spending time together but the souls' transferring has not taken place yet. Moreover, Pramod and Anurag also were not liking their meeting each other on many an occasion like that and expressed their dissatisfaction at them also. While they were worrying very much what to do, they received a phone call from Manohara Rao asking them to meet him in his clinic.

"After a thorough research I came across the real story of a couple like you who wished so much to be the opposite sex. They were also young male and female like you, living in a foreign country and they also met while they were going on a sea journey. They both have no previous acquaintance with each other but became good friends and expressed their strong wish to each other. They also were fall asleep at the same place and by the time they woke up, they found themselves in the other body! Their souls were changed into the other's body!"

Pramod and Sameera looked into each other's faces with surprising expressions. "So ours is not the only case." Sameera said and Pramod nodded his head.

"They digested their shock, took each other's contact and other details and just like you both, enjoyed their both strong desire to be in the opposite sex while managing themselves in the other body. But even after they have got their desire completely satisfied, souls' transfer into the respective bodies has not taken place. That means they could not go into their own body."

"Did they remain in the other's body like that forever then?" with a horrifying expression in her face Sameera said. "I cannot even imagine like that! I just cannot say how much I want to go into my own body now and lead life with Anurag."

"I am also feeling in the same way now. I so much want to go into my body and be together with Purnima." With a pathetic expression in his face Pramod said.

"You both did not hear me in full." With little irritation in his face Manohara Rao said. "I cut the story short. They both have been advised to do something by some parapsychologist and they did just like that. After they did it, their souls could go into their own bodies again."

"We also do it just like that. Tell us what we should do?" Pramod asked him excitingly.

"You have to tell us about that first and anything else later. What it is? First tell us about it?" Sameera was also as much exciting as Pramod.

"Without hearing what they did; you both are feeling so much enthusiastic! I am afraid whether you both do agree to it at all." With gathered frowns, Manohara Rao said.

"You are jumping to conclusions without telling us about it." Sameera said with irritation. "Don't kill us with suspense and please tell us what it is."

"After coming this far, I don't remain without telling about it to you." Sighing heavily Manohara Rao said leaning back in the chair. "They both had sex together. While being in the other body, they both had full-fledged and hard core sex. That was what suggested by that parapsychologist to them to do and how he got that idea I don't know. After that sexual act, they found themselves in their own body and never such a situation took place in both of them."

There was absolute silence after Manohara Rao said that and Sameera and Pramod looked into each other's faces with shock and uneasy expressions.

"I am not saying that it would work out but you both may experiment it if you want. But it is absolutely upto you to decide." Breaking that silence, Manohara Rao said that and remained silent as if there was nothing more than that he could say or do.

Sameera and Pramod with uneasy feelings came out of that clinic.

x x x

Pramod and Sameera would have taken more time to take that decision if Anurag and Purnima have not shown much disinterest for their meeting quite often like that. But without meeting each other as often as possible, there were so many things that they could not manage to do presenting in the other body. Moreover their desire to go into their own body has become too much strong and there was not even a semblance of their desire to be in the opposite sex in them then.

So, they have taken the decision to experiment with it as the couple in the foreign country did. They booked a room in a hotel and met in that on that day as they planned before.

"As we are having it anyhow, we do have it in the way we want. Every kink of us should be satisfied! Even our experiment does work or not, this experience should be in our hearts forever." Pramod said.

"Oh, please don't say like that! You just don't know how much I am wishing that this experiment to do work. I just cannot bear to be in the other's body anymore. If it helps, I don't have any objection to have sex with this body in whichever way you want. If you are thinking having hardcore sex will make the result more promised, I have no objection to have it like that."

With the strong desire to go into their own body rather than with the desire to have sex and rather than with the desire to satisfy their kinks but with the hope it makes the possibility of transferring of souls more, they both have sex in a full-fledged and absolute manner. They both did not know how much of time has passed but by the time they both finished it, they not only completely satisfied but their bodies were filled with sweat with the exertion they put.

"My god! I never have experienced this much of joy with anyone till this moment." Pramod said kissing on the right cheek of Sameera. "I must say you are wonderful dear."

"Among those all with whom I have it, you are the one fucked me the best I must say." Kissing on his lips straight Sameera said. "It is something I can remember forever."

With absolute naked bodies they both held each other gently looking into each other's faces and Sameera suddenly yelled observing her body. "My god! I am feeling myself in my own body now! My soul entered into my own body!"

"Yes, you are right!" Pramod also exclaimed. "I am also feeling myself in my own body! That means my soul entered into my own body!"

Sameera hurriedly got off from the bed and even more hurriedly dressed herself up. "Pramod, please don't mind I am going away from here. I am feeling fear if I stay long with you, once again our souls change place. You never try to meet me and I also never try to meet you again."

Pramod sighed heavily and remained looking at the retreating figure of Sameera. He did not try to stop her at all as he also has the same fear.

Epilogue

"There is something very important I want to tell you. And I want to tell you about it in my home in private. This is the last day we both do meet in our home." On that day Susmitha said that to Pramod. It was just the next day Pramod's soul entered into his own body.

"I am pregnant Pramod. And I am pregnant with your baby. I do love to have your baby in me." When they both met in the house of Susmitha, Susmitha said so to Pramod.

"How it is? It can be your husband's also." With shock filled heart Pramod said.

"It cannot be. We both stopped having sex together a long time back. I already told you that he has lost his sexual appetite completely and not feeling for it. He also knows that I am pregnant and feeling happy to have one more baby even though it is through you." Susmitha sighed heavily. "Anyhow it is just like satisfied all my sexual urge. Presently I am feeling only for my baby. Even you don't like it, I don't want to have it with you anymore."

"Never mind. I do like it a lot." After saying that, even without waiting for her coffee, Pramod came away from that place.

Pramod and Purnima, Sameera and Anurag were the happiest couple on the earth. Purnima and Anurag always thought their spouses' partial memory problem has been solved completely by their spending time together like that. Except Manohara Rao, no one else has known about the changing of the souls in Pramod and Sameera besides themselves. Except Pramod and Sameera, no one else knew, what experiment they did to make their souls to go into their own bodies again. Their happiness has become even more when Sameera and Purnima have become pregnant with their respective husbands.

Pramod and Sameera did not try to meet each other at all again and they did not dare to talk even through phones also with the fear that their souls may once again change place.

End

Did you love *Two Strangers On The Bed*? Then you should read *A Girl's Conflict*[1] by Kotra Siva Rama Krishna!

[2]

Sirisha who was a fifteen years aged girl and was studying tenth class, became completely upset when she came to know that her mom was pregnant and was going to give her a sibling just in some six months or so. The sudden fear which Sirisha has was; her dad could not expend amount for her medical studies while looking after another child also. Moreover she does not like sharing any of hers with another sibling either it was a brother or sister. She went even to that extent to demand her mother for abortion of her pregnancy. Because of her stubbornness and persistence, both of her parents were yielded to her demand and her mother became ready to get the abortion of her pregnancy. Just at the moment when her mother was about to have the abortion, a

---

1. https://books2read.com/u/4jq76l

2. https://books2read.com/u/4jq76l

transformation has taken place in Sirisha and she just pleaded her mother not to have the abortion and let her have the sibling. How the transformation has taken place in Sirisha, what really caused that transformation and what happened before that transformation is the story ' A Girl's Conflict' with 29,000 words.

Also by Kotra Siva Rama Krishna

Two Strangers On The Bed
A Girl's Conflict
Enna
Strawberry
Dusk
Just Relax!
Delicious Predicament
Nirupama
Half Opened Doors
Lovenest
Moonshine
Scarecrow
Closed Doors
Disturbed
Handfuls of Sand
Mansion of Illusions
Rain Flower
Rose Garden
Sand Dunes
Snow Flower
Split Personality
Being Possessed
Objection Sustained
House of Delusions
Rustle in the Leaves

Sasikala
Amaswitha
English Grammar Simplifier
Wisps of Smoke